ORLAND PARK PUBLIC LIBRARY

3 1315 00365 2836

P9-CCU-155

A Present for Mother Bear
Copyright © 2002 Nelvana
Based on the animated television series *Little Bear* produced by Nelvana
™ Wild Things Productions
Little Bear characters copyright © 2002 Maurice Sendak
Based on the series of books written by Else Holmelund Minarik and illustrated by Maurice Sendak
Licensed by Nelvana Marketing, Inc.
All rights reserved. Printed in the U.S.A.
Library of Congress catalog number: 2001092692
www.harperchildrens.com

A Present for Mother Bear

BY ELSE HOLMELUND MINARIK

ILLUSTRATED BY CHRIS HAHNER

HarperFestival®
A Division of HarperCollinsPublishers

ORLAND PARK PUBLIC LIBRARY

It was Mother Bear's birthday. She was still asleep.
Father Bear was making something sweet.
"It's my present for the party," he said.

Little Bear said, "My present will be flowers.
Mother Bear loves wildflowers."

Little Bear picked a fine bouquet.
Now he was ready to invite his friends.
First he went to Hen's house.
Hen was looking for her wreath.

"It was on the door," she said.
They looked about—no wreath was found.

"Oh, I like your flowers!" said Hen.
"They are for Mother Bear—for her birthday,
and you are invited to the party," said Little Bear.

"Wait," said Hen. "I have a picture frame.
Mother Bear will like it. Will you trade?"
Little Bear looked at the frame.
"Okay," he said. "Come along, then."

So off they went to Owl's house.
Owl was stringing beads.
He saw Little Bear's new present—
the frame.
What a wonderful frame.

"This frame is for Mother Bear. It's her birthday.
You are invited to the party," said Little Bear.
"Mother Bear would like beads," said Owl.
He wanted to trade his beads for the frame.
They were very nice beads. Little Bear traded.

Off they went to find Duck and Cat.
First they found Duck.
She was wearing a red sweater.
It was coming apart. A big ball of wool was on the ground.
The sweater had not been finished.

Duck saw the beads. "Ooh, how pretty!"
"They are for Mother Bear's birthday,"
said Little Bear. "You are invited."

Duck liked the beads.
She slipped out of the sweater—
and into the beads.
Before Little Bear knew it—
he had made a trade.

There he stood with very little sweater
and a big ball of wool.

365 2836

ORLAND PARK PUBLIC LIBRARY

Cat came out from behind a tree.

"That ball of wool," he said.

"I have to play with it. I can't help it."

"But it's a birthday present for Mother Bear,"
said Little Bear. "You are invited."

"I'll trade you this wreath that I just found!" said Cat.
"But it's my wreath!" said Hen. "It was on my door!"

So Hen got the wreath,
Cat had the ball of wool and the little bit of sweater,
and Little Bear had no present for Mother Bear.
What to do?

Little Bear shook his head.
He went off to find the perfect present
for his dear Mother Bear.

Everyone came to the party,
and the presents they gave were the trades they had made.
Now wasn't that nice?
Hen's present to Mother Bear was the wreath for her door,
and Owl's present was the picture frame,
and Duck's present was the bead necklace,
and Cat's present was the ball of wool.

And Little Bear's present was a
beautiful bouquet of wildflowers.

"Oh," said Mother Bear, "they are just perfect!"
And she gave her Little Bear a sweet little kiss.

Little Bear said, "That was sweeter than the flowers!"
"What about my cake?" asked Father Bear.
"That's sweet, too!" said Mother Bear
and gave him a kiss also.
"Hear, hear!" cried everyone.

And then they sat down to eat.
It was a grand birthday party for all!

ORLAND PARK PUBLIC LIBRARY